Lesléa Newman

MATZO BALL MOON

Illustrated by
Elaine Greenstein

Clarion Books ★ New York

Clarion Books
a Houghton Mifflin Company imprint
215 Park Avenue South, New York, NY 10003
Text copyright © 1998 by Lesléa Newman
Illustrations copyright © 1998 by Elaine Greenstein
First Clarion paperback edition, 2005.

Illustrations are monoprints, overpainted with gouache.
Type is 14-point Garamond.

www.houghtonmifflinbooks.com

Printed in Singapore.

Library of Congress Cataloging-in-Publication Data

Newman, Lesléa.
Matzo ball moon / by Lesléa Newman ; illustrated by Elaine Greenstein.
p.   cm.
Summary: Eleanor and her grandmother make matzo balls
in preparation for the Passover meal.
ISBN 0-395-71530-X
[1. Grandmothers—Fiction. 2. Matzos—Fiction. 3. Passover—Fiction.
4. Seder—Fiction.] I. Greenstein, Elaine, ill. II. Title.
PZ7.N47988Mat   1997
[Fic]—dc20   95-49577
CIP
AC

CL ISBN-13: 978-0-395-71530-7   CL ISBN-10: 0-395-71530-X
PA ISBN-13: 978-0-618-60481-4   PA ISBN-10: 0-618-60481-2

TWP   10   9   8   7   6   5   4

For my mother and Aunt Audrey
—L. N.

For Barbara Diamond Goldin
—E. G.

On the morning of Passover, Eleanor woke up bright and early and ran downstairs to the kitchen. Mama and Daddy were sitting at the table drinking their coffee.

"Where's Bubbe?" Eleanor asked. "Isn't she here yet?"

Mama put a bowl of cereal down at Eleanor's place.

"She'll be here soon, Eleanor. Come eat your breakfast."

"Is Bubbe going to make chicken soup with matzo balls?" Eleanor asked.

"I hope so," said Mama.

"I hope so," said Daddy.

Eleanor lifted a spoonful of milk from her bowl and blew on it, pretending it was chicken soup, still too hot to eat. Then she took a bite of cereal and ate it slowly, pretending it was a sweet, chewy matzo ball.

Eleanor's big brother, Joshua, raced into the kitchen, gulped down his orange juice, and ran out to catch the school bus just the way he always did.

"Don't forget, Bubbe's coming today," Mama called after him.

Then Daddy left for work and Mama cleared the breakfast dishes.

Eleanor waited and waited and waited. At last she heard the *chug-chug-chug* of Bubbe's car pulling into the driveway.

"Bubbe!" Eleanor ran outside to give her grandmother a great big hug. Bubbe was soft and round and smelled like a flower garden. "Bubbe," Eleanor asked, "are you going to make chicken soup with matzo balls?"

Bubbe thrust her hands on her hips and pretended to be insulted. "Do the leaves tumble down from the trees every fall?" she asked.

"Yes," said Eleanor.

"And do the flowers come up from the ground and blossom every spring?"

"Yes."

"And does your bubbe make chicken soup with matzo balls every year for Passover?"

"Yes," said Eleanor, "yes, yes, yes!"

"Well then," said Bubbe, "what are we waiting for?"

They carried Bubbe's suitcases into the house, and Bubbe unpacked her two special cooking pots, one for the chicken soup and one for the matzo balls.

Mama handed Bubbe a yellow apron with flowers all over it, and Bubbe went right to work. First she put a big chicken in the soup pot. Then she cut up celery and carrots and onions and put them in the pot too. Next she filled the pot with water and set the soup on top of the stove to cook. Soon the whole house smelled like a holiday.

"Now for the matzo balls," said Bubbe. "I need matzo meal and eggs and oil and salt."

Mama got out the ingredients while Bubbe filled the second pot with water and set it on the stove to boil.

"Eleanor," Bubbe asked, "are you going to help me make the matzo balls?"

Eleanor thrust her hands on her hips and pretended to be insulted. "Does the snow fall down from the sky every winter?" she asked.

"Yes," said Bubbe.

"And does the sun shine hot and bright up in the sky every summer?"

"Yes."

"And don't I help you make matzo balls for Passover every year?"

"Yes," said Bubbe, laughing, "and just for that, I'm going to make the first matzo ball an extra special one, just for you."

Eleanor helped Bubbe mix together all the ingredients with
a big wooden spoon. Then Bubbe took a clump of dough
out of the bowl and rolled it around and around between
her hands.

"This one will be yours," Bubbe said, dropping the big, fat
matzo ball into the boiling water. Eleanor watched it tumble
around. "Now help me make the rest of them," Bubbe said.

Soon Eleanor and Bubbe were busy rolling globs of dough between their hands. The dough felt soft and mushy, but Eleanor knew the matzo balls would be nice and hard and chewy after they were cooked in the boiling water.

Twenty minutes later, Bubbe lifted Eleanor's matzo ball out of the pot with her wooden spoon. It was the biggest, lumpiest, bumpiest, yummiest-looking matzo ball Eleanor had ever seen.

"Can I eat my matzo ball now?" Eleanor asked.

"Of course you can," said Bubbe. "Go get a bowl."

Just as Bubbe turned from the stove with Eleanor's matzo ball, a voice called out, "I'm home!" and Joshua came racing into the kitchen, his school books flying.

"Hi, Bubbe!" Joshua threw his arms around Bubbe and squeezed her tight. "Is that matzo ball for me?"

"No," said Bubbe, "this one is for Eleanor." Bubbe slid the matzo ball into Eleanor's bowl. "But maybe she'll share it with you."

"I don't want to share," Eleanor said, taking the bowl from Bubbe. "We made lots of matzo balls, Bubbe. Can't Joshua have one of his own?"

"Joshua, go get a bowl," Bubbe said, and she fished another matzo ball out of the pot.

"Happy Passover, everyone." Daddy came into the kitchen, home early from work for the holiday. "Don't I get a matzo ball?"

"Go get a bowl," Eleanor and Joshua said together.

Bubbe gave Daddy a matzo ball.

"Well," said Bubbe after a minute. "How are they?"

"Delicious," said Daddy.

"Nice and chewy," said Joshua.

"Bubbe," Eleanor said, "this is the best matzo ball I have ever, ever had."

"Who's going to help me set the dining room table?" Mama asked, coming into the kitchen. "My, don't those matzo balls look good." She went over to the cupboard, got a bowl, and helped herself from the steaming pot.

Before long it was almost dark and time to get ready for the Seder. Bubbe and Eleanor went into the dining room to assemble the Seder plate.

"Let's see," Bubbe said, "we have the egg, the shank bone, the parsley, the salt water, the matzo, and the bitter herbs. What are we missing, Eleanor?"

Eleanor looked at the Seder plate. "I know," she said. "We need to make the charoses."

"You're right," said Bubbe. "Go get me the apples and walnuts. They're in the fruit bowl on the kitchen counter."

Eleanor headed for the counter, but the matzo balls smelled so good, she couldn't stop herself from going over to the stove and eating one.

"I'll get the macaroons." Joshua ran into the kitchen just as Eleanor was heading back to the dining room with the apples and walnuts. On his way to the pantry, Joshua stopped at the stove. "Those matzo balls were so nice and chewy," he said to himself. "I think I'll have another one."

Daddy came into the kitchen with a yarmulke on his head, just as Joshua was rushing out with the macaroons. "We won't be eating for a while," he said to himself. "I think I'll have a matzo ball."

Just as he finished the last bite, Mama came into the kitchen for the candlesticks. "Will you put these on the table?" she asked, handing them to Daddy. As soon as he left the kitchen, she went to the stove. "I better check those matzo balls," she said, helping herself to a nice, fat one.

At last it was time for the Seder to begin. Mama lit the
candles and said the special blessing. Daddy turned to the
first page of the Haggadah and began to read the story of
Passover. Bubbe passed around a pitcher of water and a
towel so everyone could wash their hands. Eleanor asked
the traditional four questions. Joshua broke the special middle
matzo called the Afikomen and said the prayer over it.

When it was time for the Passover meal, Bubbe served the soup.

"Where's your matzo ball?" Eleanor asked Bubbe, pointing to Bubbe's bowl with her spoon.

"There aren't any left. Somebody's been eating my matzo balls," Bubbe said, pointing her finger around the table.

"I had an extra one," Joshua said. "Here, you can have mine, Bubbe."

"No, take mine," said Daddy. "I already had two."

"I've had my fill. Here, take my soup." Mama slid her bowl toward Bubbe.

"I'll share mine with you," Eleanor said, slicing her matzo ball in half with the edge of her spoon.

"Shah!" said Bubbe, shaking her finger at everyone. "Eat up, all of you. As long as my family enjoys, I enjoy. And next time I'll make so many matzo balls, we'll not only have enough for the Seder, we'll eat them for breakfast the next day too."

After they finished the Passover meal, it was time to open the door for Elijah, the prophet who will one day come and bring peace to the world. Eleanor went to the front door and opened it. She looked out at the dark night sky filled with stars and stars and stars.

As Eleanor kept watch for Elijah, the full moon began to rise. The night was so clear, she could see all the craters of the moon. *The moon is so big and lumpy and bumpy,* Eleanor thought. *It looks just like a matzo ball.*

"Bubbe, come quick," she called.

Bubbe came and put her arm around Eleanor's shoulders. "Did you see Elijah?" Bubbe asked.

"No," said Eleanor, but I found a big, bumpy, lumpy, yummy-looking matzo ball!"

Bubbe looked at Eleanor. "Where?"

"There." Eleanor pointed to the moon. "There's the matzo ball moon, Bubbe, and it's just for you."

Bubbe looked up. "My, doesn't that look delicious?" She laughed. "Let's go get our spoons." But instead of going back to the table, Bubbe and Eleanor stood together, gazing with wonder at the big, bumpy, lumpy, yummy-looking matzo ball moon.

About Passover

Passover, or the Festival of Freedom, is an eight-day holiday during which the Jewish people recall the delivery of their ancestors from slavery to freedom. On the first two nights of Passover, a special meal called the Seder is eaten. During the Seder the Passover story is told.

THE SEDER TABLE IS SET WITH THE FOLLOWING:

CANDLES

WINE (including a cup for Elijah the Prophet, who will one day bring peace to the world)

HAGGADAH (book that tells the story of Passover)

SEDER PLATE upon which is placed

roasted egg (a symbol of birth and renewal)

maror bitter herbs, usually horseradish (a reminder of the bitterness of slavery)

karpas greens, such as lettuce or parsley, to be dipped in salt water (a reminder of the salty tears Jewish ancestors wept)

matzo unleavened bread (a reminder that the Jewish people had to flee Egypt so quickly, there was no time for the bread to rise)

charoses a mixture of chopped apples, walnuts, cinnamon, and wine (a symbol of the cement made by Jewish ancestors when they were slaves)

shank bone of a lamb (a symbol of the sacrificial Passover lamb)

Many traditions are observed during Passover. All leavened bread and bread products are removed from the home and not eaten during the entire eight-day holiday. During the Passover meal, four cups of wine are blessed and drunk. Everyone washes their hands at the table. Greens are dipped into salt water and blessed. The middle matzo, called the Afikomen, is broken. Part of it is hidden, to be eaten later. The Haggadah, or book of Passover, is read. The youngest child reads the traditional four questions about why this night is different from all other nights. A bitter vegetable (maror) is dipped into charoses and eaten along with a sandwich of matzo and bitter herbs. After the Passover meal is eaten, the Afikomen is distributed for dessert. There is a grace after the meal.